SEVERED VEIL

TALES OF DEATH AND DREAMS

BETHANY A. JENNINGS

Thank you for all your support and friendship! ♡

Bethany A. Jennings

For more information on the author, visit:

www.bethanyjennings.com

Creative team:

Editing by Janeen Ippolito LLC

Cover design by LoriAnn Weldon

Formatting by Julia Busko

EARLY PRAISE FOR SEVERED VEIL

"A bold and thought-provoking collection that will appeal to fans of daring heroes and fantastical worlds. Highly recommended!" – Sarah Delena White, author of *The Star-Fae Trilogy*

"This is not just a book of stories—it's an experience... tender, merciful, empathetic rest for the aching soul." – RJ Conte, author of *Lucent Sylph*

"Each story has this sense of defiance and hope..." – Rosalie Valentine, author

"Severed Veil is a masterpiece—a vivid kaleidoscope of soul and imagination that reaches far beyond the final page and nestles deeply in a reader's heart. Jennings' gorgeous prose and unique worlds are woven through with the reminder that even in the darkest moments, light can pierce through our nightmares and ignite our courage." — Kara Swanson, award-winning author of *The Girl Who Could See*

DIAMONDS

I was not born this way,
feeling the weight of the world,
screams of the dying,
the lost,
the wounded,
like tethers pulling my heart to the darkness.
I was not born this way,
awake to a pain I've never felt,
crying for a hurt I've never carried,
weeping for what could have been,
what isn't,
what never will be.
I was not born this way,
eyes wide,
hands shaking with rage,
lungs tingling with flight or fight
that would drive me to run
if I only had an enemy to face.
But I have none.
Not a tangible enemy.
Only the mirror,
the weight,
the darkness of no hope
that whispers,
"Come hither.
You know me.
You can trust only me.
Turn to me, embrace me.
there is no hope,

there is no light.
I am your last resort.
I am all there is.
I am your homeland."
I was not born that way,
but I was born with the darkness.
I grew up
with the weight of the world
shielded away
(until it came crashing like a wave,
drowning me in shadows)
but I was born with the darkness,
quietly eating,
silently luring,
caressing my trembling skin
with promises of comfort,
if only I would turn my gaze to its depths
and block out the light.
But I defy you, darkness.
I defy your shadows,
your comfortable blackness,
your dullness,
your desire of diminishing
all that I am
into a place where I cannot see
cannot know
the pains that I cause,
the hurt I create,
the fear I inflict,
or worse, what I *could* know—
and would not care,
because I am cocooned

in the darkest of places,
where all I can see,
all I can feel
is myself.
I defy you, darkness.
The light may be blinding,
the fire burn,
the brilliance sear,
but it is Life.
It slices the heart like a blade,
it divides me from my dross,
it blazes my bones,
but it is beautiful.
My uncaring,
my dull edges,
my dimness
are filed away to knife-sharp points,
set on edge,
lit from within,
roused in a dance,
singing like an arrow.
I would rather be shot
from the bow of my Warrior-King
than sit in the dark,
rather stab shades in His hand
than be buried so deep,
rather be sharpened,
excruciatingly sharpened,
than left in a hole,
in a cave,
underground,
away from the light,

a lump of iron
smug
and useless
and comfortable.
I was not born this way,
seeing the shapes of the shadows—
for in the darkness.
all is shadows,
all is black.
I was not born this way—
I am being forged this way.
I am a shard,
I am a blade,
glinting with light cast across me.
Shadows, fall.
Darkness, flee before me.
I was not born this way,
but I will be sharp as diamonds.

HEART OF THE GIANT

I'm not ready to go back into the Sleep.

I grit my teeth, feeling the blaze roar across my soul—echoes of the destruction stalking the land. My hand slips up to my heart, then my throat.

Fire. Charring. Ash.

"Princess?" My handmaiden lowers her embroidery, leaning closer. "Are you all right?"

"He's back," I whisper. "The dragon."

Not again. Not my country.

Fire envelops my consciousness, turning everything else into a hazy blur. I can smell the smoke, and the blazing houses flicker in my mind's eye almost as vividly as being there.

I collapse. Hands lift me, carry me through the castle halls.

A wagging beard and pointed hat lean over me, and I catch a glimpse of the wizard's sharp blue eyes. "Princess."

"I can't do it," I croak.

"You have done it before, and you can do it again, your highness."

"I don't want to Sleep." I writhe, fighting against the heaviness that weighs my limbs and sucks my mind away. "I hate becoming the Giant." At least when I was young, when I merely succumbed to the nightmares for days while the dragon descended, I wasn't disappointing my country, attack after attack. Since the Giant was built for me, every Sleep ends with the despair of failure. The dragon is always bigger, always stronger. I choke in a sob.

"You have no choice." There is urgent warmth behind his gruff tone. "What was the purpose of building the Giant, what is the purpose of all your suffering, if you cannot kill the dragon and end this curse upon you and on this land? You must keep trying."

"Maybe there is no purpose. Maybe fire takes us all." I shudder, and gasp as another stream of flame tears across my soul.

The wizard and the others fasten enchanted chains around my hands and feet, tying me tight to the throne within the Giant's ribs. I shut my eyes—tears leave cold streaks down my face—and I surrender myself wholly to the Sleep, sinking into deep, dark dread and lonely wandering.

The magic coils around my body. It hums with desperate purpose, melding my soul to the Giant's heart, diffusing my unconscious mind through the frame of metal and gears. The Giant wakes, while I dream deep at its core.

I am no longer a princess—that life feels as far away as the waking world. I am as tall as a mountain. As impenetrable as a fortress. As powerful as a dragon.

I am the Giant.

Shaking my iron limbs, I rise from beside the castle gate and stare with piercing glass eyes toward the south of my realm. Charred mountains reach into the low-hanging clouds, mist weaving at their feet and thunder rolling above, but in the distance, fresh black smoke rises from a southern village. A lithe shape with broad green wings circles in the air, then swoops down to spew another river of fire.

I set off at a run, metal clanking, leaving deep craters in the moss and mud.

When I reach the crest of a hill above the village, I launch off its peak, hurling myself at the beast's scaly hide as a blade extends from my metal hand. My other arm catches the dragon by the hind leg, and I drag it earthward, slamming it into the rocks of a mountain pass. Our landing shudders through my frame.

The dragon shoots a stream of fire that heats me straight to the heart. I stagger and slice my blade across the creature's wings.

One of them severs from its back.

Its roar shakes the mountains. Fire lashes up the cliffs, blackening the rocks. The creature rips into my arm with its teeth, piercing the newly hammered metal. I pull away, tearing my own shoulder open. Magic bleeds from the gap, and my soul screams in pain within me.

The dragon stalks across the top of the nearest cliff, hissing, its red mouth open and tongue slithering out between teeth like spikes. Its nostrils flare in a sneer. Then it leaps. It slams into me and knocks me to the earth, striking my metal face again and again with its teeth.

Half blinded, I fling all my energy into a sword thrust. My weapon stabs through the dragon's open maw as it draws back for another bite. I pierce through its throat, down its neck.

It writhes in pain, slithering off of me. With a groan of laboring gears, I rise. I wrench my blade harder, deeper into the dragon's throat, until it is buried deep inside, piercing its heart.

The dragon gives a last blast of flame that torches my face and chest. And then it goes limp. I crouch frozen over its body, waiting...waiting...

Rain begins to fall, pattering on my hull.

Everything is still.

For a moment, I fear that the Sleep will last forever—that I will be a Giant for all ages, stalking my rescued country as a hulk of iron and wheels.

Then the shadows around my heart lighten, and consciousness dawns, bright and hopeful. The enchanted chains melt with the faint aroma of smoke. I rise from the throne, and throw open the Giant's back door.

Cool, wet air hits my face. Far below at the Giant's feet, villagers cheer, raising grateful hands. I smile as the damp wind plays with my hair.

My land is safe. The dragon is dead. And the Sleep will never take me again.

The fires are going out, on the hillsides and in my soul. I shut my eyes and breathe the living scent of rain.

LOYAL TO A FAULT

Technically it's illegal to be out here.

I brace my feet against the slick shuttle floor, trying to ignore the enormous fragments of space junk floating past the window. Plenty of veterans have left dead comrades in the inky blackness, but these days, with the rumors… Only Dad would be nuts enough to ask for his remains to be scattered in the old military graveyard beyond the asteroid belt.

And only I was nuts enough to bring them here.

I hug myself tighter.

Why am I even here? Mom pleaded for me to stay, for us to bury Dad normally.

An echo of his voice rings in my mind. *You're a Murberry, Tara Jane, and we Murberries are loyal to a fault.*

He wanted his remains left with his old pals from the army. And I didn't want to let him go until the very last second.

A monitor beeps on my dashboard.

That last second being now. I'm almost there.

Leaving the ship on auto, I unbuckle and tread to the back, where the wooden coffin sits. It smells like the warm dirt of our farm, a comfortable and familiar scent amidst the dankness of the shuttle. I don't dare open it and see his face—mangled by the farming equipment that took his life. But I lay a hand on the splintery top and take a deep breath. "Dad—"

The floor tilts. I slam against the coffin with a scream.

Something drags on the shuttle's wing, throwing everything sideways.

Gasping, I wrap my arms around the coffin, hoping it will keep me from sliding any further as the ship tilts. We jerk away from whatever's holding us and shoot forward, only to be caught again.

Grating screeches rebound on the ship's hull. The lights flash. As we lurch sideways, the coffin loses grip on the metal floor and becomes airborne.

Smashes into me.

Crushes me against the wall.

Flings me into darkness.

My last thought is of Mom, alone on the farm, losing both her husband and her daughter in the same hellish week.

All because I went along with this foolery.

ooooooooooooooo

I wake to the piercing smell of chemicals and pain like a reverberating gong in my skull. I'm being carried along on some smooth surface. Machines whir and clank in the faintly green dimness. The air is frigid.

I seize the sides of my bed, only for my hands to chafe on moving metal. I'm on a conveyor belt! Heart pounding, I push up to a sitting position. Brief gratitude pings in the very back of my brain—my hair would have been dragged into that belt if I hadn't chopped it all off the day after Dad got dragged into the combine.

"This one—is still—not dead."

I scream. The robotic voice came from beside me, so close I could touch the thing.

"What—shall we—do with it?" another answers from my left.

Scrambling for the edge, I snatch the knife in my overalls pocket.

A mechanical voice screeches. "Product—on—the move!"

I leap off the conveyor and slam into a fleshy hulk. Arms like ice wrap around my shoulders. The chemical smell engulfs me. Bile rising in my throat, I stab my knife into cold, thick flesh.

No reaction.

In a flash of light I see the face. Lifeless eyes. Battle scars. And a dark uniform, like the one Dad asked to be buried in.

I shove away, hollering, and run.

"Catch it!" another robotic voice shrieks.

I stagger over tools and junk on the floor, and crash to my knees. A distant window on the ceiling shows a wheeling view of stars—I must be on some kind of space station. At the other end of this long, dark room, a patch of light falls on a vehicle parked in an open area. The shuttle! I scramble to my feet again, heart racing, and terror burns in my throat as I see corpses—so many corpses—rolling past on the conveyors around me, limbs splayed everywhere, vacant eyes staring toward the knives and wheels and tools that spin down from the ceiling.

I run three paces nearer, then freeze. The back of the shuttle is open. The coffin is gone.

My breath snags in my throat. What is this place? What are these fleshy robots?

Was it illegal to come out here because of the danger? Or was this the new empire's doing, hidden out in the darkness of the void?

Maybe I can evade the monsters—find out what's really going on here.

But the creatures gain on me, feet thudding heavily on the floor. With a burst of speed, I reach the battered ship.

A hand grabs my wrist, twisting me around.

The face looks into mine. My father's face. Torn by the machinery that took his life. Eyes blank like a wiped slate. "Dad!" I scream. His arm wraps around me—like one of his old hugs, except cold and dead and ready to crush my throat if I resist.

I can't breathe.

"Here—is—the subject," his voice drones. Nothing left in his brainpan. Like something else is living through him, moving all his muscles.

Trembling takes me all over. "Dad," I croak. Maybe if I get him out of here, he'll be okay. Maybe he can recover his real self. Maybe we can escape together. "Are you in there? Do you hear me?"

He doesn't acknowledge me. Doesn't flinch. His mouth moves again. "Kill it."

Another reanimated corpse shuffles forward with a rusted blade.

One thought sings to the surface. *Loyal to a fault.*

My mother's face enters my mind—with her warmth, the farm, the sunlight, and everything I associate with her goodness—and desperate love revs me into action like fresh gas in the tractor tank. With a surge of adrenaline, I tear Dad's arm off me—or rather, what used to be Dad—and fling myself away. I trip and fall, half-running, half-crawling up the gangplank of the shuttle, and collapse just inside, slamming down the lever to lock the door.

The gangplank rises, shutting out the ambling dead who are hurrying to catch me. Their hands claw and scrape on the outside of the ship.

Someone's got to get to the bottom of all this, but Mama's not losing her whole family to the empty darkness of space that haunted my dad to his grave. Not today.

More reanimated bodies surround the shuttle as I rev up the engine. Some at the side are pulling out guns and grappling hooks. But in the distance, I see a bay door with an oxygen shield, open to deep space.

I catch another glimpse of my father's scarred face—but only for a moment, as my shuttle barrels over the drones and through the shield toward freedom. Toward life.

I'm coming home, Mama. Dad is gone, but I am coming home.

BLAZE

I can't stop the story,
the movement,
the pain,
the dancing of visuals
carved in my brain,
the eager compulsion,
that cry of my soul,
the frenzy,
the vision that's burning a hole
in my mind.
I can't shake it.
It's mine, this I know.
My quest, not another's—
for only I'm full
of *this* racket,
this chaos,
this burdening fight
of characters, stories
that scream for the light,
this rabbit hole,
endless,
that calls me to war
to fill barren pages
with worlds from my core.
And I fidget.
I bite
on my lip in the dark.
Am I a creator?

And is this my spark?
Or is this insanity?
Should I give in
to this spellbinding blaze
captive under my skin?
What if I'm deluded,
my passions misled
by this thing,
this enigma
that dwells in my head?
Am I stubborn,
a fool,
to think this could be gold?
But I'm sick
at the thought of my heart left untold.
Perhaps I'm obsessed
and should let it all go—
but a prayer leaves my lips.
and my heart whispers:

"No."

THE DISCONNECT

To RJ – this story belongs to you

Eighteen years old. Time to disconnect.

I have dreamed of this day all my life—every blink of time when my mother didn't tamp down my longing with practicality and the need for obedience.

Now I finally sit on the edge of an exam table, my feet held still so they won't swing, my arms at my sides so I won't wrinkle this beautiful, crisp yellow blouse.

The doctor's face is heavy with the gravity of the moment. "Tiffany Lewis, after your training chip is removed, you will be solely responsible for your actions. Anything you say or do that is socially unacceptable could have lifelong consequences. Do you understand?"

I nod. I'm supposed to feel cautious, maybe proud, but most of all somber about this responsibility. I will be a great adult.

"You may lose control briefly," the doctor says. "Your body is not used to moving or talking without the safeguards of the Parental Control chip. One day if you become a parent, you will appreciate how hard your parents worked to protect and guide you to this point."

I'm supposed to be grateful. I smile and nod again. I am a perfect example of good manners.

"The procedure will take only a minute."

At the side of the room, my mother smiles at me. I feel an appropriate swell of gratitude for her years of guidance.

I'm supposed to be sad now, grieving the connection we are about to lose. My lip curls in a pout. She blows me a kiss.

Latex dust flies as the doctor snaps on his gloves. His hands mess with my hair, pinning it aside with a clip.

The scalpel slits the back of my head.

I wince, but my mother and I share a glance and a smile driven by her encouragement. This will be the last time she helps me be brave and strong, she reminds me. After this, I have to do it all myself.

"I'm removing the chip," the doctor says.

Pain flashes like lightning in my skull and whips my entire body. A warbling cry bursts from my mouth.

My head pounds. The doctor grabs for me, but I tumble to the floor and collapse on hands and knees on the concrete, trembling all over. Light dances in my vision.

I have to get myself up. Nobody is going to do it for me. I can arch my back but that's about it. The world is swimming, and my insides swim with it.

The doctor's gloves snap behind me. "Congratulations, Tiffany Lewis! You are now an independent adult."

I curl over and pitch my stomach's contents all over the floor.

"Tiffy!" Too close to my ear, a high voice squeaks in wounded outrage.

Mother.

Her stiff hands drag me up, and I stand like a newborn calf, sick and dizzy with my knees bent inward.

"Your legs will remember how to walk," the doctor assures. "Adjustment will take a couple hours."

I dry heave again. "Wha…" These are supposed to be my first words, the first real words coming from *me*.

I don't even know who I am yet.

Mother puts her arm under my shoulders to steady me, and I aim a light, dizzy swat at her.

"Stop vomiting. Behave!" she hisses in my ear. Too close, too shrill. "Francie's videoing!"

She gives her friend a pained look. The woman stands nearby, holding a camera aloft.

"This is all perfectly normal, Ms. Lewis," comes the doctor's calming voice.

"*I* am not normal!" Mother snaps. "I mean, *Tiffany* is not normal. I am not one of those lazy moms. I worked hard raising her! Control your gag reflex, child," she whispers. "I can't do it for you, remember? Get it together."

I overcome the gagging shelf that feels like it's blocking my throat. Words come slow. "I…was not…me. I was you."

"Don't be silly, dear. Smile!"

She drags me toward the camera, her face filled with a wide grin. "Look at her, all growed up! Yay!" Her voice hasn't changed much since the baby videos.

Francie is filming this.

I wobble. There is blood in my hair and bile on my lip, and these legs are too long and narrow to move with this unsteady toddler gait.

She's probably streaming this to all her social networks.

I toy with the idea of retching again, this time in Mom's hair.

She wipes my mouth with her own sleeve. "Sorry, peeps! I didn't realize the disconnect could get so ugly!"

"Ugly" is this yellow blouse she had me wear. Mom wants yellow everything. I never noticed how hideous it was. I was supposed to think it was the nicest color in the world.

Mom aims her big green eyes and pointy smile at me. "Tiffy! Say something nice for the camera!"

If this is what she's going to share with all her friends, it'd better be good.

I stammer and blink. Words feel unfamiliar. "Well…my head hurts, but it's starting to clear…"

As I speak, I suddenly feel firm on my feet again.

My own two feet.

I push Mother's hands away, and lift my chin for the camera, rubbing the back of my neck. Wetness is seeping into my collar. My fingers come away red with blood.

Mother's jaw drops as I smear it across the front of my blouse.

"I'm a grown up now," I say. "And yellow is the ugliest color in the world."

SPARKS AND ASH

"I've taken your family. Your things. Your memories. Nothing left but your tattered skin. I'd kill you…" My enemy straightens. "But why bother killing a nobody?"

In the wake of her triumph, my laugh startles the silence.

"But this proves I am Somebody." I etch words into the air through my pain. My fragmented thoughts ignite – sparks on gunpowder trails. "I've altered the world. I've seen it in ways all my own. You can't erase me. I exist. Even if you burn my bones…I will exist as ash."

She seizes her axe, but I smile as it swings.

NO MORE BLOOD

Something in this sword feels...broken.

It's so perfect between my palms, the rippled steel cold on my fingers. With my own gifting, and with the skill-magic that hums through this ancient blade, I could carve down any enemy.

But memories leach from the steel, soaking into my fingers, permeating me with the bitterness of metal and blood.

"It doesn't want to fight anymore," I murmur.

Rekin's dry voice cuts into my awareness. "Well, that's stupid. What use is a sword for, if not fightin'? Kinda like what use is a prophesied savior-girl, if she's not doing any actual savin'?"

The men laugh. I flinch. Recovering the enemy's most powerful weapon still hasn't earned their trust.

My voice falters. "This blade's re-forging...it didn't ask for it."

Rekin sneers. "*Ask?*"

"Hush." Captain Tathe halts. "Listen."

The company silences, and a stick snaps between the redwoods. Rekin tenses. Hands slip toward sword hilts.

The captain's voice cracks through the air, aimed at me. "Run!"

Figures in crimson dart through the trees—burst on our company like flying drops of blood. Coming for the sword. Coming for me.

Every instinct screams for me to fight.

Run?

Shock streaks through my frame. Tathe believes me. Believes this crazy old weapon that pleads with my soul.

What use is a prophesied savior-girl, if she's not doing any savin'?

Please, the blade begs in my sweaty palms. *No more blood.*

The crimson warriors close in.

And I flee. Not looking back. Casting aside all fear of Rekin's scorn. The sword's relief pours into my soul until tears streak my cheeks. Behind me, soldiers crash through the ferns, but I am far ahead.

She shall defend the defender, the prophecies say.

But I was not born to fight with this sword.

I was born to fight for it.

LIVING IN THE LIGHT

What if I told you
        that living in the light—
          living in blessings,
        living in all my dreams come true—
doesn't stop me from seeing the darkness,
        walking along a dim path,
              crying, heart twisting,
        as I walk beside someone who's not?
Someone who's living in a shadow they can't shake,
        crushed beneath a mountain that,
          try as I might,
             I cannot move,
          cannot budge,
               cannot push aside.
So here I am, standing in the light,
  with someone I love buried in rubble.
              (Lord, let it never be real—
              real dirt, real rubble.
          Let it never be real.)
What if I told you
        that the darkness that pours from my pen
          is deeply felt,
            is crying out on behalf of another,
          not myself—
                  is that okay?
"Write what you know," they say.
  And I know what it's like
        to stand beside the heap of darkness,

crying for a loved one to get out—
(Please please please, let them out)
to wish that I could rip depression's face with
claws of steel,
but it's untouchable, just a darkness,
nothing I can grasp.
It slips through my fingers—
while it holds them in an iron embrace.
I want my love back,
I want my heart back,
but here I am,
living in the light,
calling down through the cracks,
crying, "There's light,
there's light up here,"
wishing they could only see it too.
"What do you know of darkness?"
you may wonder.
But rest assured,
one can live outside the grasp of darkness,
one can live out in the light,
one can live in glorious bounty,
but still be a survivor.

THE DESTROYER PRINCE

For Brittany

The screams of the dying are a distant whisper on the wind.

Here by the mirror pool, hidden in the cleft of the mountains, I can barely hear the chaos, the aftermath of what I've created. I release my mare to graze, and sink down onto the sand beside the rippling water.

My hands are red with blood—but not my own.

Nothing shall harm him.

The fae called it a gift. For me it is a curse.

Soon the company will find me, drag me back, parade me through the streets, and send me out for another bloodbath. If there is time, perhaps I will snatch a scant night's sleep—haunted by the screams of villagers I've slain. A shudder of loathing rolls down my spine.

No more. The invincible hero will be their slave no more.

Moonlight glints on my knife as I raise it to my wrist.

"Don't."

The single word cuts the air like a crystal blade. I startle from my seat on the damp sand. "Who goes there?"

A head rises from the water, hair dripping in thick braids like weeds—or perhaps they *are* weeds. Shoulders follow. Then a naked torso, pale as paper in the moonlight. She is as delicate as any of the women who were thrust at me in the courts, before my brother slit his own throat. Before the gift fell to me.

Around the woman's narrow waist, glints of steely scales reflect the water that hides her lower half.

I shiver, feeling rooted to the ground. Mountain merfolk bewitch travelers, luring them into ponds and drowning them, dragging them into their watery caves. But surely she cannot hurt me.

The blade edge brushes my wrist, and I remember what I was about to do.

"Don't," she says again, softly.

"Because you prefer your meat alive?" I whisper. "Why do you care what I do?"

Her weedy hair shifts as she tilts her head to study me. "Because you matter."

"Of course I matter. I'm the damned Destroyer Prince!" Bitterness floods my tongue. "I'm tired of mattering. I want to not matter. To be free."

"You are afraid." Her silver voice threads through my head, sending out tendrils of keen curiosity.

"Nothing can harm me but my own hand. I have nothing *to* fear," I growl.

She gestures toward the knife. "You have visited this pool since you were a boy. But since the curse fell to you, when you visit, you always sit with your knife and look at your wrist—hesitating. How many times has it been? Five? You are afraid. Because you know that you should not."

"Is it wrong to kill myself when I know hundreds will die by my hand tomorrow if I do not?" I cry. "This is my country and my mother its queen. What else is there for me but this?"

"What enslaves you, prince?" Her moss-green eyes pierce me. I know better than to lock gazes with a mer-fae, but I cannot look away.

The green consumes me, dragging answers from my depths like a net drawing in dark fish. "I am enslaved to my warmongering mother. To the people. To the songs they sing of my legacy, though I've only begun to be this destroyer they exalt. There is no life for me outside of that. Only disgrace. At least in death I will not face disgrace."

When did I enter the water?

The coolness ripples around me, flooding into my boots, soaking my breeches and tunic. I stand waist-deep in the pool, now, and the merwoman's fingers trace down my arm to my hand...and gently draw the knife from my bloody fingers.

Her green eyes meet mine again, tender and searching. "There is always another way."

The blade melts in her hands and blows away like a wisp of smoke on the wind.

"Their songs will change," she declares. "Now they will sing of the Lost Destroyer Prince. The hero who disappeared."

Sudden fear thrums inside me. "If you have the magic to kill me," I croak, "do it. But the curse will pass to my cousin. It will never end. Even your people will fall, if the queen has her way."

"What seems to be a curse now may be a gift later." She nudges me into the deeper waters, leaving barely a ripple on the surface. My own movement creates a splash that frightens a nearby night-bird into the treetops.

A shout rises from the grove beneath the mountain cleft, and a stab of alarm pierces my heart. They've found me!

"Your people drag men into your caves, and drown them," I whisper.

"Not you, prince." The mermaid shakes her head.

Scaly hands grasp me from every side, dragging me deeper. A shout of panic rises inside my chest, and I move to wrench away from their grasp, but their cold grip is too tight.

Water closes over my head. The moon becomes a rippling, shapeless blast of white trickling into the pool.

"No more," the princess says—for now I see the row of sparkling horns like crystal daggers across her brow. The crown of the mer-fae queen. "No more lives will be lost tonight, my prince.

Not even yours."

Her voice comes clear to me, even in the water as it surges past, as they draw me down to their caverns. A faint lilt of music rises in the current.

I can breathe.

"Did you not say," the queen sings in my ear, "that nothing could harm you but your own hand?"

I reach one last time toward the surface, toward the life I have known—and in the rush of pure mountain water, I see the blood flowing away, dissolving into the pool like my dagger vanishing in the wind.

My hands are clean, and I sink downward, falling toward the distant sound of mermaid song.

AETHERWORLD

I stop at sunset.

In the wilderness, all is silent except the rustle of trees. Swaying on aching feet, I glance up the deserted road, then down a hillside into a valley below, where sweet-smelling grass ripples in the warm wind. This is far enough from civilization. It will be safe—for a moment—to check the Aether for Nyam.

I pull the little elixir bottle from my pocket. Only a few drops shimmer in the bottom now, and without training, this tiny vial of magic is my only way to reach the Aetherworld.

I sink in the grass, uncorking the bottle, and tip a single drop into my dry mouth.

My body collapses. Like sand trickling through an hourglass, my soul slips from it, drifting into the secondary Aetherworld.

It overlays the physical realm like a rippling curtain of gauze, coating the world in gray as far as the horizon, and it has valleys and mountains all its own, dipping and climbing in and out of the physical world in unpredictable ways. I can still see the physical realm beneath, but it feels distant and muted.

The Aether is so cold and empty—not even sunlight. I forget how harsh this hidden world can be, reflecting my emotions in its weather.

Soul travelers would glint golden like dust motes on the Aetherworld's canvas. I see none. My hopes sink. *Please, my love. I risked my life and left everything for you,* I plead. *Don't abandon me now.* In the dreams, Nyam promised to come to me in the Aether and lead me to the border, to freedom.

What if the dreams weren't real at all? What if it was just my heart, longing for the lover my master sold to another trader three years ago?

Gossamer wings unfurl from my back, lifting me. I smile, and suddenly the Aetherworld feels warmer for it. *At the very least, I will be free. Then I will be able to harness these powers and take them into the real world too.* Until I cross the border, my master's spells hold me back from full command of the Aether.

A figure appears over the hill. My heart leaps—and then chills. This isn't another soul traveler. It's a striding, breathing man, coming over the knoll above where my body sleeps. He is no elf, no Aether warrior.

Panic stabs through me. Until the elixir wears off, I'm helpless in the physical realm. My limp body is hidden well enough in the grass to escape the eye of a casual traveler, but if he is a slave hunter…

Light catches on a hunter's medallion pinned to his upper arm, and the Aetherworld crusts over with the ice of my terror. *No.*

He stands at the crest of the hill, scanning the landscape with a hand on his knife. Then he plows his way down the slope, into the vale. Perhaps if I remain in the Aetherworld long enough, he'll just pass me by…

I'd be almost as helpless with soul and body united. What could I do against a hunter?

My arms and legs tingle. The otherness that separates soul and body is tangibly dissolving. In a moment I'll melt back into oneness. I thrash in the Aether, desperately hoping against hope that with no training, no assistance, despite the limiting slave spells, I might take my gifts through the crossing. With wings I could escape him! On those tired feet, I am doomed.

He's within yards of my still body now.

I frantically cling to the wings in my mind, willing them to stay on my body.

But then I sift through the gap again like sand, soul trickling back to reunion with my body. The wings dissolve. I moan in despair—and my heart leaps in terror.

The sound left my physical lips too.

The hunter bears down on me before I can rise.

"Please!" I scramble backward in the grass. "I'm just a traveler—just a—!"

His powerful hand pinches around my arm. "You lie, *elf.*" He speaks the name of my enslaved race with contempt, and painfully flicks my pointed ear for emphasis. "Playing in the Aetherworld, are you?" He tears the vial from my hand.

"No!"

"Does your master know you stole his elixir too?" Like a wave too powerful to resist, the hunter drags me toward the road.

My legs burn to bear my weight, but I'm drowning in a sea of sorrow broader than the expanse of the Aether, and I barely feel the pain. *Master will bury me in spells so deep that Nyam will never find me again, even in dreams.*

A shadow darkens the ground ahead.

The hunter shouts in surprise. My gaze whips toward the hilltop.

Nyam descends on the hunter with a shout, hair flying, blades of Aether magic flashing like sunlight in his hands.

The hunter shoves me aside, and I slam into the grass with a gasp. Above my head, he unsheathes a glinting blade, ready to strike down Nyam as he comes—

But I hook my foot around the hunter's booted ankle, and yank. He stumbles sideways. His blade falters.

And Nyam embeds a sun-bright sword through the man's chest.

The hunter crumples to the earth. Nyam releases the swords

from his hands, and they vanish like sparks into the air.

I gape.

I'd almost forgotten what he looks like outside the shadows of the Aether. Dark hair curling to his strong shoulders. Bronze skin a shade darker than mine. Dark eyes with that lively spark in their depths. And gentle, calloused hands, now both held out to me.

I take his hands—and leap up to kiss his perfect mouth as his warm arms warp around me.

When I finally step back from our embrace, I tilt my head up to look at his face. "I thought you said only souls could travel in the Aether!" I exclaim, still holding his hands tight. "How did you get here?"

Nyam grins. "Come!" He leads me toward the top of the hill, and my legs carry me, sore but filled with the new strength of hope. "I couldn't leave you to travel on your own," he says. "So I came on foot."

A shiver runs through me. "If the hunters catch you again—"

"They won't. And if they do...we'll be ready." His eyes glint at me. "I can start teaching you to use your powers *now*. With your hand in mine, you don't need potions. You don't need dreams."

I blink, and my mouth falls open. The Aetherworld suddenly stretches out before us, even as we run. Its folds shimmer iridescent, filled with a relief and happiness I have never seen there before.

Nyam and I are together. And freedom is waiting.

Joy floods my veins. My feet fly lightly across the grass as, for the very first time, my delicate dragonfly wings unfold in the warmth of the sun.

HOPEBRINGER

I am Hopebringer.
Ray of sunlight cutting through a dark place.
Golden, set up on a stand.
Reflective.
They see what they want in me.
And I was happy
to step into this role,
to meet expectations,
a symbol of life,
of hope,
of deliverance.
I doubted,
but something inside me
was so confident,
so certain,
that I was Hopebringer,
that I had that capacity, that essence inside of me—
but now I'm not so sure.
Because the more they trust,
the more they hope,
the higher I rise,
the greater the stakes—
the darker I become.
Optimism rusting over,
turning to ash.
I'm a golden veneer,
I'm a deceiver,
A false savior.

I am lost.
And if I could find the words,
I would tell them:
Please,
no,
it isn't me—
You want Another,
One so strong,
so capable,
so unbreakable,
not this shell of a man
breaking under the weight of the chains
that some consider glory.
I can't bear it.
Too heavy.
I can save no one.
I am scarred, flawed, shattered.
But here I am.
Here I stand, in the flesh.
Alone, save in Spirit—
that Spirit inside me.
If I am His hands and His feet,
then what does that make me?
Where does that leave me?
Is this what it means,
to be a broken vessel?

DREAMSKIP

To those who feel unheard, and those who dream of courage

I sense Harriet entering my dream before I see her.

Suddenly everything is too loud, too sharp, looming around me. Broken glass scrapes under my shoes, and when I glance down, streaks of blood blossom across my arms and hands. The busy theme park in my dreamscape dissolves away—now I stagger half-naked down an empty hallway that's closing in on me like a trap.

Fear squeezes its fist around my heart. This is the part where I want to wake up.

I have to make myself stay long enough to talk to her.

I turn to all sides, hunting for my schoolmate. Dreading how she might manifest this time. "Harriet?"

"Milo."

And there she is in front of me, her shoulders crooked, her hair a mess of dark chaos, her nightgown drenched in red. Scrapes and bruises mottle her pale face.

This is even worse than last night.

Through the veil of sleep, I'm vaguely aware of my teeth clenching, my heart racing, my sweat dampening my sheets. I'm on the verge of waking. I have to talk fast. "Harriet, you're dreamskipping wrong again."

Tears stream over her bruised cheekbones. "Don't leave!" She trembles, blood dripping from her hair. "You're the only one who can save me."

I shake my head, trying to appear firm and brave, even though all I want is to run away to reality. "You can't bring your dream into my dreams like this. That's not how skipping is supposed to work. You're projecting your fears and giving *me* nightmares."

"It's not a projection. I need you."

"If you're scared, then wake yourself up!"

She whispers back, her blue eyes wide. "Waking up is worse."

My fear sparks into irritation. "What is going on? I wish we could just talk this out during the day." I haven't spent much time around the kids in the special ed class, so I don't know why, but Harriet is mostly nonverbal in real life, among other things. Discussing this in person is probably impossible.

Harriet sucks in a deep breath. Holds it. Lets it out slowly. "Milo, if you do not intervene, I am going to die."

"You keep saying this, but you haven't told me *how* I'm supposed to 'intervene,' or when, or where!" I cry.

Harriet opens her blood-stained mouth—

The jarring blare of my alarm clock hits like a hammer across my brains. I awake with a gasp, drenched in sweat, squinting from the bright beams coming through my window.

Crap. There's no getting that dream back. I rip aside the bed sheets and stalk toward the bathroom, grabbing my jeans off the nightstand.

It took me awhile to realize that Harriet was a fellow skipper. When she first started visiting my dreams, she always brought such a painful and warped perspective of the world with her. I thought I had effectively taught her how to control her skips— how to slip alone, seamlessly, into other sleepers' minds, without dragging her entire subconscious into it. For any skipper, that's a challenge. I thought I'd helped her master it.

But here she is again, painting my dreams into worse and worse nightmares, leaving me shaken.

I lean on the bathroom counter and sigh at my disheveled reflection. Things can't go on like this anymore. I have to try to communicate with her in real life. Somehow.

I stride into school with forced determination.

Jamin sees me slam my locker shut, and looks at me with one eyebrow quirked up. "What's with you this morning?"

My willpower shrinks a bit at the prospect of what I have to do. "Has anyone seen Harriet Linnow?"

"Who?"

I sigh. Nobody even recognizes her without the cruel nickname the other kids inflicted on her for her wild hair and unpredictable moods. "Scary Harry?"

"I dunno, man." His frown deepens across his dark forehead. "My girlfriend helps with the special needs group, and she mentioned Harry didn't get dropped off this morning like usual. Why are you looking for her?"

My stomach tightens. It's hard to imagine discussing this with Harriet herself—who by day barely acknowledges anyone else's existence—about how she's shown up in my dreams all weekend, bloody and broken, begging for me to save her. Surely, *surely* she knows what she's up to in her sleep. I remember all my skips! But she can barely form words. Even if I talk to her, how will I know if we really understand each other?

Whatever's going on...it seems serious. And she's not here.

I let out a breath from low in my gut. What if those bleeding wounds and disheveled clothes aren't a subconscious fear or a cry for attention? What if she's getting brutally injured, in real life, right *now?*

I know where she lives.

Urgency floods my chest, and I look Jamin firmly in the eye. "Tell the teacher I had an emergency and had to go." I spin on the toe of my sneakers and sprint for the door.

His bewildered voice echoes down the hall after me. "Milo?"

I shove aside the school door and pelt down the steps.

For five long blocks of sidewalk, my shoes madly slap the pavement. My mind reels with fears and possibilities, my throat burning from exertion, cold wind stinging my face.

Anything could be happening to Harriet. I could be running headfirst into anything.

And this isn't a dream.

I've skipped into the dreams of black belts—trained from them without their waking knowledge. I've visited the dreams of psychologists—sat quietly and listened to their lengthy rants. I've challenged a bully—in dreams, taught him a lesson he won't forget. But out here, out in life, I'm still a weakling.

Out of shape. Out of breath.

Out of time to think.

I scramble to a stop in front of the Linnows' barred front door. The glass is cracked, the screen door behind it ripped. All the curtains are drawn. Something feels wrong about the whole place.

Anxiety creeps down my spine, and I divert to the cinderblock wall alongside the house, where I quietly lift the latch of the gate and slip into the side yard, hoping no neighbor will call the cops on me. Once inside, I drop and crawl along the patio to the backyard, where I tuck myself between an unkempt potted shrub and a back window. Ever so slowly, I rise up until my eyes peek above the windowsill.

Dark red smears stain the wall across from me. Broken lamps. Pictures ripped down from the walls. Is this Harriet's room?

My throat constricts. I cast my gaze across the bed.

Empty.

I fiddle with my phone in my pocket. Should I call the cops? On what grounds? *This girl keeps appearing in my dreams, sir, and telling me she's in danger. Oh, and we haven't really talked about it in real life because she can't talk.*

I look back to the stains of red in the room. It looks like someone's head has been bashed repeatedly against the drywall. I swallow. Who am I to be snooping around, spying, making these assumptions?

She's trusting me. She's relying on me.

Why me?

Because she can only communicate in her dreams. And I'm the only one who knows—sometimes the people in your dreams really see you, really hear you. Even if nobody else can.

Okay. Here I am, Harriet. I take a deep breath. Where are you?

Glass shatters somewhere at the other end of the house. The hair on the back of my neck stands on end. I hold my breath.

Then distant wailing. Pleading. A male voice growling back.

I creep out of the bush, dial nine-one-one, and shove the phone back in my pocket on mute. Every muscle in me is clenched in fear.

I try the rusty back doorknob. Unlocked.

Buzzing with nervous energy, I ease open the door and step into a hallway. Drops of blood stain the beige carpet. Harriet's?

My throat tightens, but I keep moving. The sound of weeping grows louder with every step—and then the tinkle of broken glass scraping on kitchen tiles.

"Shut it, you," the male voice mutters. Vicious. Threatening.

If only I had a weapon.

I ball my hands into fists. The words of the martial arts teacher come rushing back. *Tuck your thumb beneath your fingers, not wrapped inside them, or it'll get broken. Angle your hand down, so when you punch you're hitting with your first two knuckles.*

I reach the kitchen doorway.

Harriet stands at the kitchen sink in nothing but a long pajama shirt, bleeding welts smeared down her bare, spindly legs, and massive knots in her hair. She moves in short, jerky motions like a zombie, like every step hurts, as she sweeps broken glass into a heap.

I turn my gaze toward the man in the corner. Middle-aged, muscular, unshaven. He sits in an untied bathrobe, hunched over a bowl of cereal. A belt rests beside his dishes, like a man in an old western might keep a revolver handy.

Bile coats my throat.

The man's gaze leaps to me as I enter. "Oh—shit! Who are you? How did you get in here?" He jumps to his feet, snatching a knife from the nearby counter.

Harriet startles and turns. Her distant eyes are like circles of blue ice in a face ringed with dark tangles. In waking life she's never looked me in the eye before.

The man seizes her by the hair. The broom clatters on the linoleum as she buckles under his hand, whimpering and clutching at her head.

He sneers. "Come any closer and I'll cut her!"

I thought nothing would come out of me but a raspy, terrified breath. That there was nothing inside me but fear. But rage drives me—boils my soul to flames until the words come out with a roar. "If you don't let her go, I will pound you into the wall!"

In a millisecond he sizes me up—

And I lunge.

The next thing I know, I'm standing over his still body, my head light as air, my hands shaking and burning with pain. I stagger back and clock my head on the edge of the table as I collapse.

Slowly, like a distant siren coming closer, Harriet's wails

reach my addled thoughts.

Or is that a real siren?

I lift my head, woozy.

From the other side of the kitchen, Harriet looks up. She's sprawled, quivering, still clutching her head among the shards of glass. Her ice-blue eyes fix on my face. Then on my arms.

I look down and see blood.

So much blood.

Oh. Oh, God help me. I collapse on my back under the table. Help me, help me... Deep breaths, deep breaths.

I can't.

I can't.

Darkness descends like a blanket thrown over my consciousness.

∞∞∞∞∞∞∞∞∞∞∞

Harriet, did I die for you?

It was worth it. You were worth it. None of this dreamskipping matters if I can't use it for something good, like saving a life—

"You didn't die."

My muddled dream solidifies into a vision of a garden I remember from my childhood, and Harriet approaches through an arbor, wrapped in a blanket over a hospital gown.

A smile twitches on her lips. "I'm just two floors down and one door over. You're in what they called...the ICU? Both of us are sleeping. Obviously."

I process it for a minute. "And you're okay?"

"As right as I can be." She sits down on a garden bench and curls the blanket around herself.

I sink to a seat beside her. "What happened to you?"

She shrugs. "My mom brought him home after a date on Friday night. She never did have good taste. He killed her. Then he was going to kill me, but he decided to keep me instead."

My heart twists. "Why did you come to *me* for help?"

She blinks. "Here in my sleep, when I skip, I can explore and dream and do things. And talk to boys, like you." Harriet winces. "But most of them aren't nice boys. They won't talk back. Not the ones who know me. They're just disturbed to see me, and treat me rudely. You can tell a lot about a person by the way they treat people in their dreams." She smiles. "But you talked to me nicely, until you got scared."

Sorrow winds tightly in my heart. If I'd listened to her sooner, I could have cut her suffering short. But I'd held back, resisted, tried to push her fear and misery away.

I cast my gaze down at my arms, layered in bandages.

Harriet reaches out tentatively and brushes a hand across the gauze, her voice timid. "I'm sorry he did that to you. I didn't know you'd actually...*come* to help."

"It's nothing!" I shake my head hard. "*Nothing* compared to what you've been through. It's an honor to bear these scars for your sake."

Cautiously, gently, I take her smaller hand in mine.

She rocks forward and back again. "In the daytime, when I wake, I'll be the same I always am. I won't talk. I won't eat."

I hold her hand more tightly. "I won't leave you."

"I will cry a lot."

"That's okay."

"And maybe hit people."

I smile and stroke her thumb with my finger. "It won't scare me away."

Harriet bites her lip. "You *told* me to go away. To stop coming to your dreams. Is that what you want?"

"No! No. I'm sorry. I didn't understand—I should never have

said that." I wrap my arm around her frail figure, tucking her blanket tighter. "Whatever life is like in the waking world, no matter how many people drive you away, or hurt you, you can always share my dreams with me. Every night. As long as we live."

"Promise?" Light dawns in her blue eyes.

"Promise. And in the waking world, I'll try to make sure you are safe," I add. "I can't control the world of dreams, any more than reality, but I *can* promise you this. I will always defend you, awake or asleep."

The distant beeping of a monitor stirs my consciousness. I feel the dream fading, letting me rise toward day—toward light, toward pain.

"I'll visit you in the morning," I whisper.

Harriet breaks into a smile as she slips away. "I'll visit you in the night."

ALSO BY BETHANY A. JENNINGS

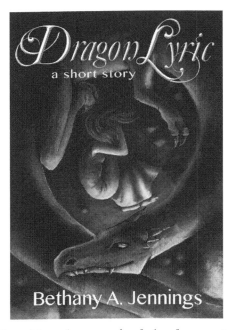

Her husband is a dragon. And the dragon is hungry.

Drawn by his allure, Theryn left everything behind to live with Roth in his mountain cave. But then her fiery-eyed husband transformed into something else: a monster of scales, claws, and wings. The dragon has only one use for her—to bear his dragon egg, now forming in her womb. After the egg is laid, she will be nothing but fresh meat.

But Theryn refuses to suffer the same fate as Roth's former brides. For her own sake, and for the baby dragonshifter she carries, she must find a way to escape the monster, and break the enchantment of the dragon lyric.

What happens when your gift turns against you?

All her life Bess has known the magic streams around her, waves of power she can draw from to wield the gift of magical threads. Now the youngest member of a team of Anchors, she helps protect the city streets from Drifters—energy thieves who prey on the life force of ordinary humans.

But when a battle leaves Bess's threads in an irreparable tangle, she is faced with an agonizing choice: sever her threads and lose her magic forever—or be slowly consumed by her own power.

COMING SOON!

A girl who can't die
and a guy with healing powers
are the ultimate crime-fighting team…
until someone takes off with her head.

Well, here I am. Dead.

I stare down at the shallow grave, where my charred remains have been abandoned, mid-shoveling, the blackened bones protruding from the soil.

Frustration fills me. I wasn't even given a proper burial. Thugs.

"I can't deny it, Mel," says Wesley, rounding the dump site. "This is the deadest you've ever been."

Normally I'd riposte something back to shut up his cheeky Scottish brogue, which is far too cute for his own good, but right now I feel like I'd get a lump in my throat.

If I had any throat left.

"Took me awhile to find myself," I say softly instead—resenting that I must speak through my friend's neural pathways instead of with my lips. But I'm always amused by the shiver he gets when I slip through his mind like a knife. It's not quite pain. More like a startled delight mixed with fear.

He sighs. "And it's gonna take me awhile to raise you, too. I wish I could do it right now, but after all that running…"

Of course. He needs sleep, and to recharge. He isn't a miracle worker.

Well, he is. But there are miracle workers and then there are… miracle-miracle workers. Wesley is one of the former. The non-supernatural kind. Human. Just with perks. Like being able to heal any wound, even his own, with the touch of his fingers—and being able to bring one particular girl back from the dead.

OVER MY DEAD BODY: A NOVELLA

Releasing in 2019

ABOUT THE AUTHOR

Bethany A. Jennings is a YA fantasy author, sandwich aficionado, and star-loving night owl. In addition to her work as acquisitions editor at Uncommon Universes Press, she is a freelance editor and graphic designer, and also runs #WIPjoy, a popular hashtag game for authors. Born in SoCal, Bethany now lives in New England with her husband, four kids, zero pets, and a large and growing collection of imaginary friends.

Thank you so much for reading Severed Veil!
Please consider leaving an honest review—
reviews are one of the best ways to help and support authors.

Connect with the author:
Website: bethanyjennings.com
Facebook: search for "Bethany A. Jennings"
Twitter or Instagram: @simmeringmind
Quarterly newsletter: eepurl.com/dfERDb

**Join Bethany's Facebook reader group
for sneak peeks of upcoming stories, giveaways,
conversations, and other fun:**
Search for the group "SimmeringMindReaders"

33669086R00038

Made in the USA
Columbia, SC
09 November 2018